I Love You!
A Bushel & A Peck

taken from the song "A Bushel and a Peck"

words and music by

Frank Loesser

pictures by

Rosemary Wells

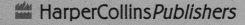
HarperCollinsPublishers

Thanks to Rochelle Schiffbauer and Larry Rakow at Kidstamps, and with special

thanks to Johanna Hurley

—R.W.

I Love You! A Bushel & A Peck

Taken from "A Bushel and a Peck" from *Guys and Dolls*

Words and music by Frank Loesser

Manufactured in China by South China Printing Company Ltd.

www.harperchildrens.com

Library of Congress Cataloging-in-Publication Data is available.

ISBN 0-06-028549-4 — ISBN 0-06-028550-8 (lib. bdg.)

Typography by Martha Rago

2 3 4 5 6 7 8 9 10

❖

First Edition

For Alexia Cable Hain
—R.W.

I love you,

a bushel and a peck,

A bushel and a peck

and a hug around the neck,

Hug around the neck
and a barrel and a heap,

Barrel and a heap
and I'm talkin' in my sleep

about you.   About you?

About you!

My heart is leapin'!

I'm having trouble sleepin'!

'Cause I love you,

a bushel and a peck,

y'bet your pretty neck I do.

Doodle oodle oodle,

doodle oodle oodle,

a-doodle oodle oodle ooo.

I love you

a bushel and a peck,

a bushel and a peck

and it beats me all to heck,

Beats me all to heck
how I'll ever tend the farm,
ever tend the farm
when I wanna keep my arm
about you.
About you?
About you!

The cows and chickens
are going to the dickens!

Doodle oodle oodle,

doodle oodle oodle,

A Bushel and a Peck

Words and music by **Frank Loesser**

Light Bounce Tempo

G	D7	G	D7	G	A7

I love you a bu - shel and a peck a bu - shel and a peck and a
I love you a bu - shel and a peck a bu - shel and a peck tho' you
I love you a bu - shel and a peck a bu - shel and a peck and it

D	D7	G	Em7

hug a - round the neck Hug a - round the neck and a bar - rel and a heap
make my heart a wreck Make my heart a wreck and you make my life a mess
beats me all to heck Beats me all to heck how I'll ev - er tend the farm

Bar - rel and a heap and I'm talk - in' in my sleep a - bout you_____ a - bout
Make my life a mess yes a mess of hap - pi - ness a - bout
Ev - er tend the farm when I wan - na keep my arm a - bout

you_____ 'Cause I love you a bu - shel and a peck y' bet your pur - ty neck I do_____

(Optional Duet)

Doo - dle oo - dle oo - dle   Doo - dle oo - dle oo - dle a- doo - dle oo - dle oo - dle ooo._____   _____